**To all my great teachers
at Emerick Elementary**

little bee books

A division of Bonnier Publishing
853 Broadway, New York, New York 10003
Copyright © 2016 by Henry Cole
All rights reserved, including the right of reproduction
in whole or in part in any form. LITTLE BEE BOOKS is a
trademark of Bonnier Publishing Group, and associated
colophon is a trademark of Bonnier Publishing Group.
Manufactured in China   LEO 0216
First Edition  10 9 8 7 6 5 4 3 2 1
Library of Congress Cataloging-in-Publication Data
is available upon request.
ISBN 978-1-4998-0181-1

littlebeebooks.com
bonnierpublishing.com

# Eddie the BULLY

## Henry Cole

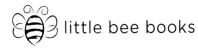 little bee books

# Eddie was a bully.

A great

big

bully.

He was mean any way he could be, any time he could b

"You're such a loser!" he clucked at Rose,
when she came in last.

"That was an easy one!" he said with a laugh, when Tony had trouble with a math problem.

You were born in a roach motel!" he sneered at Russell.

**He hid Anthony's homework.**

**He splattered paint on Melissa's art project.**

**He tripped Emma as she was getting on the bus. And off the bus.**

**"Fat!"** he jeered.

**"Skinny!"** he jeered.

**"Average!"** he jeered. Nobody was safe.

He was a good reader, but nobody wanted to sit anywhere near him during Library Time.

And nobody tagged him during Person-Person-Monkey

"He's mean," Angela said to Marco.

"Really mean," Carmen said to Sam.

"Really, really mean," they all agreed.

He was mean any time he could be,
any way he could be.

"I've had enough!"
Miss Henshaw said, ruffled.
"Time out, Eddie!"

"I've had enough!"
Mr. Fowler said, peeved.
"Time out, Eddie!"

"I've had enough!"
Ms. Cluckner said, exasperated.
"Time out, Eddie!"

**But during time out, Eddie thought of other mean things to do.**

One morning, Miss Henshaw made an announcement. "Class, we have a new student starting today," she said.

"I want all of you to make her feel welcome." She glanced at Eddie. "*All* of you."

**The classroom door opened.**

"Class, this is Carla," Miss Henshaw said.
She pointed to an empty desk.
"Carla, you may sit right there."

All eyes were on Carla as she
made her way to her seat . . .

right next to Eddie's.

"Uh-oh. Here it comes,"
Amy whispered.

"Carla's going to get a red
zinger," Tony whispered.

"Eddie's going to let her
have it," Ben whispered.

Everyone held their breaths.

Carla squeezed herself into her desk.

Eddie's eyes narrowed.
He grinned an evil grin.
He opened his mouth to speak.

"I LOVE your SWEATER!" Carla gasped,
feasting her eyes on Eddie.

"My . . . huh?" Eddie stuttered.

"I can TELL you have GREAT fashion sense!"
Carla continued brightly.
"Us FASHIONISTAS should stick TOGETHER.

Eddie blinked, glancing down at his sweater.
It *was* his favorite.

"Hey—let's do LUNCH!" exclaimed Carla. "I noticed on today's menu that we're having mac and cheese. I LOVE mac and cheese!"

"I . . . I love mac and cheese, too Eddie said, feeling a little excited

Then whoever gets to the cafeteria FIRST saves the OTHER a SEAT!" Carla squealed. "OKAY?"

"Uh . . . okay," replied Eddie.

"I bet EVERYbody wants to be YOUR friend," said Carla.

Eddie gulped. His face felt hot. "Uh . . .

"You probably get picked FIRST for teams
ALL the TIME!"

Eddie glanced around the room.
The whole class was looking at him.

Eddie felt miserable.
Suddenly he wished he hadn't been so mean all the tim
He wished he hadn't made fun of Tony in math class.
He wished he hadn't spilled paint
all over Melissa's picture.
He wished he hadn't called everybody names.

He wished . . .

he wished he could start over!

"It's really tough being the new kid," said Carla.
"Will YOU help ME make FRIENDS?"

Eddie brightened up. "I'd LOVE to!" he cackled.

Carla beamed at him.
"I knew you'd be a good friend," she gushed.

Eddie felt something.
Something inside.
Something good!

It felt *good* to be nice!

He smiled.

A great
big
smile.

**And from then on, he was a good friend—**

**any way he could be, any time he could be.**

## Dear Friends,

It's been a long time, but I remember my elementary school
as a happy place. We had great teachers.
And all of my classmates got along well, except for one.

Eddie.

Mean? Yes! Fought with the teacher? Yes! Used bad language?
Yes! Was I scared of him? Oh, yes!

Then one day our teacher made us work in small groups. We were creating
reports on the United States, and my group was assigned West Virginia.

And guess who was made a group leader? Me.

And guess who was put in my group? Eddie!

Eddie scowled at me, because I was in charge.
I was supposed to tell him what to do!

I was nervous, but I asked him to make a picture graph, showing the
different kinds of things for which West Virginia is famous. To my surprise,
Eddie began to draw a long line of freight train cars, loaded with coal.

His coal cars were perfect! Each one was dark and detailed, looking like
they were inching down a West Virginia mountainside. Eddie was talented!

I said, "Wow. You're really good, Eddie!" And he smiled.
It was the first time I'd ever seen Eddie smile.

During our group project, Eddie wasn't such a bad guy.

The report on West Virginia was an astounding success,
with much credit going to Eddie's beautiful picture graph.

Over the years I lost touch with Eddie, but I like to think he's perched
on a mountain, with paints and an easel, and the sun is coming up.

-Henry